Other Books by this Author

Enlisted at 14... A Memoir

Enlisted at 14...And the Journey Continues

Willow...A Novel

Just a Dream

Willow...and the Medusa

Enlisted at 14...Looking Back

Meet Ruben Kane

For: Willie Helyn, my mother,

You'll Love this one.

Chapter 1

In a warehouse on the east side of Cleveland Ohio, in the middle of the floor two people were tied to chairs. The man and woman were sweating profusely since it was in the middle of August. The two were blaming each other for the mess they found themselves in. The man's name was, Lawrence Robins. White, 48 years old 5 foot 8, and 205 pounds. He wore goatee and had a long straight nose. His eyes were very cold looking. Lawrence was the CEO of an up and coming business that scammed the elderly out of their homes and life savings. Time and time again the law has pulled him in but with big money. Connections and lawyers always seemed to come out of it smelling like a rose. Meanwhile; his victims were left with only Social Security while he dined at the best restaurants, drove the finest automobiles and flew to countries near and far. The homes he lived in were some of the most expensive in the country. While the woman his (secretary) and lover played the game right alongside of him. Twenty four years old and five foot four, the secretary's looks were something out of vogue magazine. She had shoulder length red hair, and baby Jane set green eyes with a long straight nose. Lips that was wide full and lush Due to recent lip surgery. She had a long slender neck, breasts the size of small cantaloupes and waist you could put two hands around. She had Wide hips and legs as long as totem poles. If there were men around she was sure whatever trouble they were in she could get them out of. She called the victims, she set them up, and they trusted her. But now they had to pay. That's when Willow walked in with Dolores right behind her; they were both black, 5'11 and were wearing high heels which put them at a little over 6 feet tall. The skirts they were wearing hit them at thigh high level. If you had to put a label on them you could call them amazons. Once the secretary saw them she knew they were trouble.

They both held a 22 revolver with a silencer on it.

"Who are you people and what do you want with us?" Robins asked.

"You really don't know?" Willow said.

"Hell no I don't know," "I'm a respectable businessman and this is my secretary. I have no idea what the hell you want", Robin said.

"Well I'll tell you." Willow said. You took the homes, money and future of some good people. We want it back."

"I assure you I don't know what the hell you're talking about and we don't have a Thing that belongs to anyone". Robin said.

We're not here to debate this with you, are you going to pay the money back?

"No! Hell no so you can just release us right now".

Willow turned toward the secretary, "what about you? You should know about as much as your boss".

"I have nothing to say" the secretary said.

Willow glanced at Dorothy and then she shot Robins in his leg. Robins screamed in pain and the blood started coming down his leg. "You bitch! He said." You bitch!"

Willow looked at the secretary and said. "Let me ask you again, where is the money."

The secretary was so shocked that she could hardly talk.

"Where is the money? "Willow asked again and pointed the gun at the secretary.

"Don't say a word!" Robins screamed, "They're not going to kill us so keep your mouth shut."

Dorothy then shot Robins in the other leg, "it's

your turn next!" Willow told the secretary.

"Wait! Wait!! "The secretary said. "The money or most of it anyway is in the Cayman Islands in a numbered account." "What is the account number"? Dorothy asked" 376921" the secretary said and there is a password. Dorothy left the room and came back with a laptop. After getting the bank she asked the secretary for the password. After transferring the money over to their account Dorothy asked the secretary where the rest of the money was. "There is no other money" the secretary said. Meanwhile Robins was moaning and crying." Let me ask you again" Willow asked the secretary, "the rest of the money, where is it?" "There is no other money that's all there is," the secretary said. Willow walked behind Robins and shot him in the back of the head. The secretary screamed and screamed until Dorothy walked over and slapped her in the face." Is there money you haven't told us about?"

After collecting the rest of the information about the money Dorothy shot the secretary in the fore head." Think we got it all?" She said to Willow.

"We got all I think there is," Willow said. Agent Jenkins should be happy about this.

A week later Willow was sitting in a small outdoor patio café in New Orleans, Louisiana drinking a cup of cappuccino and eating Danish at 8:30 in the morning. She was regrouping from that last operation Dorothy and she was on. All and all it didn't go to bad. It took us about two weeks, Dorothy returned to the Bahamas and she decided to come to New Orleans. Could have waited till Mardi gras time because it's hot as hell around here now. Willow spotted an old man a few tables away. He wore a Straw hat Louisiana style, a White shirt was worn outside his white shorts that were knee-high and he wore sandals; no socks. He was 6 feet one about 180 pounds. Creole, that's what Willow guessed. A man who was black; but his appearance looked white or there in between. He looked to be in his late 50s or early 60s either way, a fine looking gentleman. Willow could see herself with a guy like that even though she knew he probably couldn't do much for her. One never knows. Willow was a black woman but you could say more red than black. That could be partly because of the black foot Indian blood in her veins and Creole or both. Oh well, maybe one day she'll give a fellow like that a shot. She finds herself giving to charity now and then. At that moment a lady of about his same age walked up to him. She was a Chinese and black mix willow thought. 5 foot three or four, black hair cut to a Bob style. Eyes slant and nose short and wide. Her Lips were straight and thin.

The southern straw hat she was wearing was plantation style and covered part of her face and her neck. Her dress was a kaki strapless pullover which reached her knees. She wore Sandals and bare legs. Her purse hung by a strap over her left shoulder. The gentleman stood as she approached the table and they embraced. Not like lovers but more like sister and brother or friends. The waitress came over and she ordered. Willow always did have the curious mind so she watched them to try and figure them out. In approximately 15 minutes of them talking in what seemed like a hush-hush tone. A small Fiat came down the street at a slow rate of speed. The right side passenger window was rolled down. Willow saw this and thought this was peculiar since most car windows were up because of the heat and them having on their air condition. As the Fiat got near the patio Willow saw a silencer sticking out the window and pointing in the direction of the couple, before they could fire Willow yelled out," GUN! Hit the ground!" The couple immediately hit the ground but the other customers just looked around not knowing what to do; that got two of them dead. The occupant in the car opened fire with what Willow knew was an AR 15. 30 rounds were fired in all, three customers were wounded and two dead. The couple Willow warned were not hurt but tables and umbrellas were all over the place. The dead and wounded were lying about among much blood. The women were crying and the men were moaning and crying.

Ambulance could be heard in the foreground and

the people in the café were out trying to help who

they could. Willow was picking herself off the

patio floor when she noticed the couple she had

warned leaving the area when the man stopped,

turned around and came back over to her. Without

saying a word he handed her a card, squeezed her

hand and left. Willow looked at the card. It said,

Jefferson P Chachere, Attorney at Law. Its Phone

number was 761 – 336 – 4617. Address was 761

Vine St., New Orleans, LA. Willow thought maybe

I'll call him and find out what this is all about.

Before the Ambulance and police got there Willow

decided to follow the couple and leave the area. No

sense putting yourself out there when you don't have to. Back at the hotel on the 20th floor Willow had just finished taking her shower. She put on her shorts, halter and sandals. She walked over to the fridge and took out a bottle of sweet tea, set on the couch and turned on the noon news. The incident was the headlines and on the TV it looked worse than it really was, but then it's not like she waited around to have a good look. The couple right behind me both were shot, the guy behind the lawyer died and one other was wounded. They have no idea who did the shooting or why. Willow had an idea who the target was but didn't know why. Maybe she'll find out.

 The next afternoon at approximately 2 PM Willow phoned the lawyer and told him who she was and he asked her if she could come down to his office. They made an appointment for the next day at 11 AM.

At 11 AM Thursday Willow was in Chachere office. It was a midsized business in a middle-class neighborhood, 10 story office building with his being on the eighth floor. The lounge had two couches and three lounge chairs. There were a couple of end tables, magazines and a TV. There was a desk over in one corner with a middle age secretary behind it. Willow told her who she was and that she had an appointment.

Ms. Willow" the secretary said, go right in Mr. Chachere is expecting you. Chachere's office was half the size of the lounge, nice sized desk, two lounge chairs set in front. One couch was sitting on the left side of the wall. Contemporary paintings adorned   three sides of the wall and right behind the desk where he was sitting; a large picture window looking over a park. Chachere was wearing a white summer sport coat with dark trousers and shirt to match open at the collar. Ms. Willow it's really nice to meet you and thank you for what you did for me and my client, I don't know how I'll ever be able to thank you.

"It's quite all right Mr. Chachere really, I'm glad I could help in some way. Willow said.

Call me Jefferson or Jeff, after all you did save my bacon the other day.

And you can call me Janice Willow said. Please sit down; Jeff pointed to one of the chairs in front of his desk. I guess I owe you an explanation about the incident the other day. Well I was kind of curious to why someone would try and kill you or were they after your client? Willow said.

"Why don't I start from the beginning?" I think that would be better". Jeff said.

About two weeks ago Mrs. Yen came into my office and needed my assistant.

Mrs. Yen was the housekeeper of Mr. and Mrs. Geezer, she happened to be passing by their bedroom door (that was partly open) when she saw Mrs. Geezer shoot and kill Mr. Geezer.

The wife noticed the housekeeper at the door right after she shot her husband and tried to convince her not to say anything and that there would be a large sum of money in it for her. Mrs. Yen agreed to keep quit.

The murder got covered up and Mrs. Yen went on the run thinking something wasn't right after two attempts on her life, now three attempts. I guess the wife had a change of heart. She came to me and I contacted Mrs. Geezer (the wife) she admitted to nothing. Now; she knows that I know, so now it looks like she has to knock off the two of us. Via, the attempt on our lives at the café.

You know that may be way more information then I really need to know, why are you telling me all this?

Because Janice you see, I know who you are. Jeff said. The reason I set this appointment at this date and time was to find out as much as I could about you. And before you ask how I did this I'll tell you this. I've lived in New Orleans all my life and I know a lot of people. It wasn't to hard finding out new people in town, especially one who looks like you.

Since you seem to know everyone in town then you should have no problem knowing who it was in that Fiat that tried to blow you away. Willow said.

There are a lot of new people coming into town all the time. Given time I could probably find out but with me ducking and hiding I have to protect my own ass now.

And where do I come in, you said you know all about me. Willow said.

You're ex-military, Air Force, you were recruited by the FBI a few years ago. You do odd jobs for them, a troubleshooter you might say. Your immediate boss is agent Jenkins. You sometimes work with a Dorothy Malone and a male name

Jesse. You like running, martial arts. Is that enough for you?

You've been busy for just a couple of days. Willow said. Who else knows what you know? Willow asked. No one. Just me Jeff said. Okay, so what can I help you with? Willow said. Help me keep Mrs. Yen alive and might I add, me too. Jeff said.

Since you know all this about me then you know how I do things, you all right with that? As long as you can keep Yen and I alive then however you do it is okay by me. And there will be a payday in it for you, even if it has to come out of my own pocket.

Okay I'm in! I'll want to move out of the hotel I'm in and in with Mrs. Yen. What about you? Willow asked. Oh I'll be all right; there are lots of places I can go until I can get this mess straightened out. What if you can't convince Ms. Geezer to call off the hits? Willow asked. Then Janice I guess you'll have to do what you do, Jeff said.

 Willow departed Jeff's office two hours later after finding out the location of Mrs. Yen's digs and what he expected of her. On the way to check out of her hotel since it was lunchtime she thought she'd stop and get a bite to eat. She spotted a quiet lunch diner with a patio but decided she'd dine inside this time. Seafood gumbo, fried frog legs and hush puppies, maybe a margarita. Since I'm in Creole country; might as well try some of the cuisine. I May never get out this way again.

Willow entered her hotel room. After she closed the door, she was hit immediately with a blow behind the neck that she felt down to her toes. She stumbled over a stool and fell backwards to the floor. She fell on her right arm which was caught behind her back.

"Welcome to New Orleans" jackco said. Listen!

Jackco was about 36 years of age, height 5 foot 10, weight 225 pounds. Race was Creole with straight hair with a ponytail. Light skin, protruding forehead, medium nose with sunken cheeks. Light beard with inch long hanging diamond earrings in both ears. Knee-high jeans with cowboy boots, Saints football jersey and Tattoos covering both arms. Jackco was the local enforcer working for whoever would pay him.

You are getting yourself involved in something that you want no part of, there are planes leaving town all the time, you make sure to be on one.

And if I'm not? Willow said.

Jackco walked over to her and kicked her in the side, Willow fell back and jackco started to kick her again. As his feet came near her head she caught it with her left hand and came across with her right holding the knife. She cut jackco inside his right knee. He screamed and hit the floor, Willow got up and kicked him in his side. You bitch! Jackco said, I'm goanna really hurt you now!

Jackco got off the floor and started advancing and lumping toward Willow. Willow thru a karate kick to jackco's cut knee and he screamed and went down to that knee again. Willow advanced and kicked him in the head. Getting off the floor this time jackco dived at Willow who at this time had maneuvered herself in front of the open patio doors. When jackco attacked Willow this time she sidestepped and as he was going by she took hold of the seat of his pants and shirt collar and help him thru the patio doors and over the railings. He screamed all the way down, all twenty floors. There was a swimming pool below the patio but it was 20 yards to the left of where he landed, He missed it.

Willow took her knife and cleaned it off and put it back in its scab behind her back. That blade had saved her ass a number of times. I think now would be a good time to check out.

CHAPTER 2

"I think Mr. Chachere called you about me?"

"Yes," yen said. Come in.

Jeff had sat yen up in an area by lake pots- a- train in a lower-class neighborhood, in what you would call a shotgun house. Open the front door and you could see all the way through to the back. One thing that was good they had those air-conditioners running. They believe in those things down here. Being August you sure needed them.

Willow was wearing a wide bream straw hat, strapless halter and Capri tight pants with strapped sandals and she was still hot.

Once in the house that changed, cool, cool. Miss yen ask Willow if she wanted anything to drink and she replied water will do.

I'll give you bottle water because the tap Water takes a bit of getting used to. Mrs. Yen said.

Since we are going to be here together for a while I think you should call me by my first name Mrs. Yen said. It's Cora. And you can call me Janice. Willow said. After being shown to her room and Willow putting up her one bag but keeping her purse with her, she went back in the front room and she and Cora set down. Cora asked Willow how much Mr. Chachere had told her. Willow told her everything she knew except the fact that now the hitters were after Jeff too. She didn't think Cora needed to know that, she had enough to worry about. I guess I should have gone to the police first. Cora said. But she (Geezer) sounded so sad, and her husband was dead. She just pulled me in. And then there was the money. Once she got from under by saying there was a break-in and all, she figured I was a loose in. After the so-called accidents I figured out what was happening and knew I needed help."

I never did get paid.

That was blood money anyway. Willow said, no good will ever come of it. That night Cora cooked dinner, red beans, shrimp Etouffe smoked Salmon plus a bottle of red wine, Cora was a good cook. After dinner they watch a little TV and after the late-night news they hit the sack. The next morning Jeff called on the land line to the house, Willow picked up.

How is everything going? He asked. So far so good Willow said. I arrived here yesterday afternoon after checking out of my hotel. Speaking of your hotel, I heard someone fail or jumped from there. You wouldn't know anything about that would you? Jeff asked.

Maybe! Willow went on to tell Jeff what happened.

How they got on to me I don't know, Willow said.

Well the punk that went over the balcony won't be

a big lost to anyone he has a rap sheet as long as

your arm. The authorities won't waste much time

on him. Jeff said. Meanwhile I found out who Miss

Geezer's contact Man is and he's the one that's

getting these hit men, he's also advising her. His

name is Thad Thibodaux. He has a fleet of shrimp

boats and they say he also runs drugs and as you

would have guessed it, Geezer is his old lady.

Then we have to convince him to back off Willow

said.

Easier said than done, I hear he's a hard ass and

once he gets something in his head he's gone with

it. He has a number of people that work for him that does anything he says so unless something is done about it they will keep coming, Jeff said. My next step is to try and contact him and maybe he'll somehow see the light.

Good luck Willow said. Meanwhile what do you want me to do?"

Just sit tight and I'll get back to you. Jeff said.

3 PM that same afternoon Willow was in the back of the house using the restroom, Cora was in the front room watching TV when Willow heard a loud explosion that shock the very foundation of the house. Smoke filled the house and Willow ran to

the front room (what was left of the front room)

looking for Cora but knew what she'd find before

she got there. The whole front part of the house

was gone and looking around Willow didn't see

Cora until she looked up. Cora had been blown to

the top of the room that was still standing. Half of

her body was on the roof and the other half was

hanging down in what was left of the front room.

The Front door and big picture window, they were

both gone. Couch, TV, lounge chair, demolished.

The last time Willow had seen something like this

was in Kuwait.

That's when the fire started and she smelled gas,

she looked up at Cora again shook her head and

walked to the back of the house. She gathered her

things and left out the back door. Six hours later

Willow called Jeff. Have you heard? She said.

I have, Jeff said. Are you sure she's dead?

I'm sure! Didn't take them long to find us. Willow

said. Maybe jackco wasn't alone when he came to

my hotel room. If that was the case then it wouldn't

have been hard for them to follow me.

Well that's water under the bridge now; do you

think you are safe? Yes, I got completely out of

town to a place called New Iberia; do you know

where it is?

 Sure do, how did you ever find that place? That's

way out.

I thought until I heard from you I should make myself scarce even though they got their target. Do you think they'll still come after you? Willow said.

I don't know but I'm third-party hearsay now, with Cora gone I'm no real threat. He may try to hit me just for spite and I still feel I have a client. I'm going to approach him and not Mrs. Geezer this time to find out where I stand.

You think that's a good idea? Willow said.

Maybe, maybe not but I can't keep ducking and hiding, besides I still have to live and work in this town Jeff said.

How are you for security Willow asked?

I've got this 300 pound 6 feet five Samoan that I've known since childhood, he'll be there. And if it doesn't work out for you? Willow asked? I've opened you an account in Harrisburg Pennsylvania at the Ben Franklin Bank, your name with this password, the date you entered the military. If something does happen to me you can leave town, collect your money or stay around and do what you do. Other than that nothing's changed just wait for my call.

I'm sorry about Mrs. Yen Willow said," I was beginning to like her."

That's life Janice, stay safe! Jeff said.

Hello, Thad, this is Jade, I heard on the news there was a bombing out in the fifth Ward do you know anything about that?

"Yeah", Thad said. Your troubles are over now.

I heard only one body was found didn't you tell me there were someone with Cora, what happened to her?

I don't know jade but I don't feel she's any threat to you because she wasn't the eyewitness.

I don't care Thad if she's alive I want her dead, I won't be able to rest until then. We don't know what Cora told her and what about the lawyer, what are you doing about him?

First the girl Thad said. I don't think she's a threat but if you want it done then I'll see to it. As for the lawyer, I talked to him and he feels it's all over since his client is dead and hoped I felt the same. I told him I did but to tell you the truth I'm really not sure. I think the housekeeper told him everything but I don't think he can bring it forward to the cops. Your word against his and a dead woman, we'll see. Well, okay Thad I'll leave it up to you, you've done a great job up till now. Have you any idea where the other woman is that was with Cora? No, but I do know she's nothing to play with, I sent jackco over to her hotel room to show her the way to the airport and the next thing I hear is him being thrown off the 20th floor balcony. Don't know where in the hell the lawyer recruited her from. If she's still in town we'll find her, Thad said.

What you think Jeff, the big Samoan said. You think you're off the hook? Hard to say A.K., Thad is a gangster he thinks like a gangster. If he feels this will come back on him, I don't think he'll hesitate. He says he's willing to let it go but then again I may have gotten it all wrong. The wife may be calling the shots and if so... If he tries a hit anytime soon then we'll know.

A few days later Willow was driving through the countryside in

The rented jeep sport Cherokee. She stopped at an old plantation that looked like it was right out of Gone with the Wind. They had tour guides so she thought she'd sign up. The tour took about 45 minutes but it really wasn't bad, going through the house seeing how the people live back then. A lot

of things she didn't know like when people come to

visit you a flower was put in their room, a certain

color flower. And when you overstayed your

welcome they put a different type flower in your

room meaning it was time for you to go. Or the one

about the servants, the kitchen was in another

building about 20 yards from the house and when

the servants delivered the food over to the main

house he(the servant) would have to whistle so that

the people in the big house would know he wasn't

eating the food on the way. Damn, that had to be a

hard life. The people in the big house look like they

live pretty well! Willow made one more stop at a

Creole home, it also had a tour guide. Creoles were

some little people; going from room to room she always had to bend over. Her being 5 feet 11 she was told the average Creole was no more than 5 foot five. She got to wondering then, I wonder how tall Napoleon was? After that She drove up on the mound that held the Bayou, now that was something. They say that all of New Orleans was in a bowl, water all around it. Don't know if I could handle that. On her way back to her motel near suppertime on the back roads, they were all back roads around there. She was stopped by the local police. The officer who stopped her was a female and just about as tall as Willow but not as heavy. She had everything a cop was supposed to have, the hat, the shirt that was fitting where it was supposed to. Willow saw that it looked like she didn't have a vest on, all her she guessed. The cop wore a Regular utility belt. She had handcuffs a Glock and Taser gun. She had Extra clips for the Glock and a whistle. All on a set of hips that were up there with willows herself. The pants were actually shorts on two long tanned legs. The heat played hell even on the cops. I guess. She couldn't get away from the shoes, typical cop!

She must have been half everything, Willow thought she saw white, black, a little Indian and Creole, a gumbo. That must play hell on her birth certificate; all these people are half something down this way.

"I guess you're wondering why I stopped you." she said. "Yes that did cross my mind." Willow said.

You have a backstop light out can I see your driver's license and registration please? Willow gave her license and told her the car was a rental. The officer went back to her squad car and five minutes later she was back. Why are you here in New Iberia Miss Watson? Just visiting and sightseeing Willow said. This is a nice area; New Orleans is a little too fast for me.

Where are you from the officer asked? Lompoc, California have you ever been there? No, I can't say I have, said the officer. And where are you staying? Report day motel Willow said. They have a nice diner and cocktail lounge why don't you come by and have dinner with me sometime, and maybe show me around.

I just may do that, (looking at the driver's license) Jackie. And how long do you plan on staying in our town Jackie? Oh I don't know officer.

Call me Doris, Doris Gentry.

Well Doris that depends a lot on you, Willow said. You see, one knows the other. And Willow felt she knew Doris.

Well Doris said why don't we start with that dinner, say tomorrow night about eight?

When Willow return to her motel room she thought about the cop. She knew there was nothing wrong with her tail light, she had notice the cop earlier that day and she was just biding her time until she could find a time and place to stop her. The officer it seems have a thing for same-sex romance and I have nothing better to do, so...Le-Say lay bohn Tomps roo-lay (Let the good times roll).

CHAPTER 3

The cabin Willow was in was an individual one setback and away from the others. But together about 25 of them they were called a motel, I didn't get that but I guess they have their reasons for calling it that, they charged enough.

Willow turned over in the bed and before she got

up kiss Doris on her breasts, Doris grabbed her and

said. Don't get up! There are times a girl does have

to go to the restroom. Willow said. Now is one of

those times.

Oh, alright Doris said but don't be too long. And

Willow got up nude, Doris watched her backside.

I never noticed that earlier she said.

 Notice what, Willow said?

That Tattoo on your butt. What is that?

What does it look like? Willow said.

Well, it looks like some kind of face, back up a second so I can get a closer look.

Willow did what Doris asked her and returned to the bed.

Doris took a closer look. That looks like a medusa, well I'll be damned. I never saw a tattoo of a medusa before. Why did you ever get such a thing?

For just that reason Willow said. No one has one.

You also have a ring with a medusa on it, I saw you wearing it. What does it signify?

One day I'll tell you about it, maybe. Now I really do have to go potty. After Willow came out the bathroom Doris said she had to go.

Don't go anywhere she said to Willow smiling.

Willow laid down on the bed on top of the covers and put her hands behind her head and under the pillow, she was still naked. Three days with Doris and they've all been great, she lived up to the old motto that police have, protect and serve. She really served. Doris was a great tour guide to, all and around New Iberia and Lafayette even made a trip over to Baton Rouge. She'll remember this trip for a long time to come.

Suddenly the front door flew open and an albino midget stood there with a pistol in his hand, he looked to be no more than 5 feet tall. He was only about 98 pounds. Large bald head, big red eyes, Round short nose. He wore a Blue T-shirt with

Spiderman on the front and yellow jeans, and the pistol pointing right at Willow.

Are you Willow? The midget asked. The shooter had been told that there were two women in the cabin and the one who they were after was named Willow. If he couldn't determine who was who then to kill them both.

No, Willow said. "I'm not her." At that moment Doris came out the door in nothing but a towel wrapped around her middle and the little man said then you must be Willow and shot Doris in her chest. Before he could turn his weapon toward Willow he felt something in his throat and he dropped his gun and grab at the knife that was protruding from his atoms Apple. His eyes got a lot bigger than they already were and he looked at Willow in disbelief. Her arm was still extended toward him in the throwing stance. He dropped to the floor still grasping the knife trying to pull it out of his throat. Blood was coming out his nose, mouth and throat. Willow ran over to Doris and found she had been shot in the chest right over the heart but she was still alive. Willow got a towel and put it over the wound and tried to comfort her. Doris was awake and said to Willow," friend of yours"? Willow didn't answer.

 Doris, I'm going to have to leave you but I'll call 911 and they should be here soon.

"Will I ever see you again?" Doris asked

 "No! "Willow said.

"Is Jackie Watson your real name?"

"No! "Willow said.

"Are the police after you?"

"No! "Willow said.

Willow kissed Doris lightly on the lips and started retrieving her things not forgetting the knife from the little man's throat, cleaned it off and left.

Jeff this is Willow, I haven't heard from you everything still good? No, Jeff said. I was shot the other day and I'm in the hospital now. I got hit in the Hip, I guess Thad had second thoughts. At least the shooter won't have a job anymore, A.K. caught up with him. He admitted everything, of course we already knew most of it. The wife is calling the shots and Thad is just the puppet. Damnest thing is besides Thad; she has another poor sucker on the side just playing his po ass.

If he knew I'm sure he'd take care of her and the other guy, Willow said. What about leaking it to him?

Too late, Tebo was the other guy and A.K. took care of him, Jeff said. What a circus, the wife going with the hit man who boss is the wives lover.

"Damn what a mess," Willow said. So where does that leave us? And by the way who's watching your back? Where's A.K. now?

He's outside my hospital room, I'll be all right.

"That's what you said the last time, I think you

should let me handle things from here", Willow said.

"Are you still in New Iberia, you never said," Jeff said.

No, I'm back in New Orleans something came up in New Iberia and I had to leave in a hurry.

I was watching the news and I saw where they had a killing their and a cop was involved, the cop died. You don't happen to know anything about that do you?

I'll never tell, Willow said. Shit happens!

Thad, just what the hell are you doing it's been over a week now and there is still no news about that situation I asked you to take care of? You still on the job? Look Jade get off my ass, since I got involved with you and your antics my business has gone to the dogs and I've lost three of my best men.

 And who would that be Thad, you never said anything about losing anyone to me. Wait a minute you did tell me about Jackco but that's only one. Who are the others? Well there was Cid, you remember him, the little 5 foot bighead albino, I'm going to miss him, and he would do anything you ask. And then there was Tebo he...

Wait, hold it a minute, you mean Tebo is dead? Tebo? Jade said. Yeah, Thad said. We just got the news this morning, he was found dead in his car with his neck broke. I don't know how they were able to get that close to him. Jade? Jade, are you there?

Look Thad I have to get back to you, goodbye.

Well, what the hell, Thad said. She act like Tebo was her man or something, hell he was just hired help. Hated to lose him but he knew the score. Shit it wasn't like he never made a hit his self, after all he did bomb the housekeeper's pad even though he did miss the other one. And he also tried to hit that lawyer, he fucked that up to. A guy that fucked up that many times should get in a new line of work anyway. Guys like him are a dime a dozen, fuck him! I guess I'll have to go after the lawyer myself but I thought maybe I'd be able to smack attack him, would have worked too if Tebo would have done his job. I'll tell you (he said to himself) good help is hard to find.

 Jade stayed by the phone a full 10 minutes crying her eyes out before she got up and went over to the liquor cabinet and poured herself a large whiskey, straight. She drank that standing up. Poured another, set down on the couch and cried some more. She had been going with Tebo for as long as she was with Thad and that was hard to juggle husband to Thad to Tebo, it worked for a while until Robert (her husband) found out about it, that's what the fight was about, the killing and the death of four other individuals. Plus; the two at the café. Oh, I almost forgot that cop in New Iberia. Oh well, I still have Thad, Bastard!

Thad laid back on his lounge chair on the deck of his yacht, swimming trunks and a baseball cap on his head with Foster Grant sunglasses. A martini was in the cup holder on the arm of the chair. Two of his men were doing this and that and bull shiting with each other then one of them said, will you look at that! The other deckhand looked and said got damn! At that moment Thad look to see what they were looking at. On the deck of the yacht next to them was the most stunning black woman Thad had seen in a very long time. She was black but looked to be more red then black, maybe part Indian. She had to be at least 6 feet tall, hair cut short wearing a wide straw hat and wide sunglasses. Her swimsuit, what there was of it, was one of the skimpiest Thad had ever seen. She wore a Halter that covered her breasts but only her nipples. She wore a wrap that covered her butt or between the cheeks of her butt, there was some kind of tattoo on her right cheek. Her legs were long and muscular like she did some kind of exercise or was a runner or something. She was doing what they call Chan-kea or some kind of routine. By this time Thad had set up in his chair to get a better look. He agreed with his men that she was some kind of a woman.

Ralph, go over there and ask the lady if she would like to come over and have a drink with me.

You don't have to ask me twice boss, Ralph said.

He departed Thad yacht and over to the yacht the girl was on and asked could he come a board? The lady said No!

Look lady it's not for me but Mr. Thad Thibodaux (my boss), you've heard of him haven't you? He owns that yacht right next to yours. He wants to know if you'll have a drink with him Ralph went on.

"Where is he?" The lady asked.

He's the guy with the cap on looking this way. Thad knew that they were talking about him so he waved.

Tell you what, the lady said, tell him I won't come over there but he can come over here.

CHAPTER 4

Thad walked over to the ladies yacht, introduced himself and asked her name, she said Jackie, Jackie Watson from Lompoc, California, had he ever been there before? Two hours later Thad was at the wheel of the yacht and the lady was behind him and had her arms around his waist. Thad was never heard from or seen again.

Hello Ralph this is Mrs. Geezer, have you seen Thad? He hasn't called me in three days .is he trying to duck me? If so I'm not standing for it. Now if he's there I want to talk to him right now.

No, Mrs. Geezen he's not here, we're looking for him to. The last time we saw him was at the dock and that was three days ago. We've got everyone out searching for him, the business is going to hell without him. Well when he does show up tell him to get his ass over to the house ASAP.

What do you think Ralph said? Asking piggy, the other heavy. I don't know we saw what we saw but should we tell anyone he left going down river with that black girl. I can't believe that the woman took him out. Ralph said. But let's go back a minute to where this all started. Mrs. Geezen kills her husband, the house keeper witnessed it. Mrs. Geezen wanting to put this hit out on the housekeeper and asked Thad to do it. The lawyer gets involved and the attempted hit at the café. And who can forget the woman at the café sounding the alarm saving there asses. The woman at the café meeting with the lawyer, jackco following the woman to her hotel. And finally; not forgetting the situation with Jackco being thrown off the twentieth floor balcony. Tebo following the woman to where the housekeeper was stashed, the bombing by Tebo, killed the housekeeper but misses the other woman. Tebo try to hit the lawyer, missed and someone broke his damn neck. Then we find out where the other woman is, send Cid and he ends up dead. Tell me something, Ralph said? Has anyone really had a good look at this woman we've been chasing? I get the feeling that the black broad on that yacht Thad got on was her and if that's the case then I don't think we'll be seeing Thad again. I also think the hunted has now turned into the hunter.

 In that case piggy said, Mrs. Geezen will be next, are you going to tell her?

Hell no, Ralph said. She got a lot of people killed all because she wanted to drop her drawls to every Thad and Tebo. She gets what she gets

Janice, where you been, Jeff said. Your phone has been dead or you just haven't been picking up. You all right?"

 I'm fine Jeff just had to get away for a while, what about you? Any more hits on your life?

No, there hasn't, from what I'm hearing things are pretty quiet around town. Thad seems to have disappeared; no one's seen him in close to a week now. They say Mrs. Geezen pitching a bitch looking for him. You didn't have anything to do with that did you? Willow didn't answer.

Looks like a guy named Ralph has taken over even if he does return. You think he has any interest in taking over where Thad left off Willow asked?

No, I don't think so, he didn't have a dog in this hunt. That was all Thad and Mrs. Geezen doing.

There is Geezen, she's still around and could still be a threat by getting another sucker.

I don't think so Janice, let's just let it go. Jeff said.

Famous last words Willow said. You out the

hospital yet?

 Yes, I'm at home, I let A.K. go. I think I'll be okay.

 I'll see you in a few days Jeff, stay safe!
Janice, let it go!

Jade walked into her parlor from an afternoon of

shopping. Whenever she's down she likes to go

shopping. Some people like to drink, some likes to

snort and smoke weed, she likes to shop. It's The

Same feeling, maybe a better feeling. Although it

May have been better to have Thad do the buying

but no sign of his ass in over a week. No one seems

to know where he is, he could be hiding from me.

Tired of my shit I guess. I'll have to go a little

easier on him from now on. Once she had put her packages down she noticed a black woman sitting over in the corner in one of her favorite French chairs having a drink. The white cap she wore had a long Bib to it, hair just barely showing underneath. The earrings were at least half an inch long with the face of something that Jade couldn't tell. But it was silver, necklace the same color and style, large ring on her left index finger. She wore a White lace shirt see-through and a silver belt around her waist. Her pants were white Capri with white wedge straw shoes. Silver chain around her right ankle, her face looked more like an Indian than a black person, she was stunning. What are you doing in my house, sitting in my favorite chair and drinking my booze? And who the hell are you?" Jade asked?

"I'm Willow! I believe you have been looking for me, I'm here now!"

Jade's mouth dropped open and she just stood there, shaking. Willow put her drink down, pulled her p- 22 out of her purse and then the silencer and screwed it on and held it on her lap.

Because of you a very nice lady is dead, two innocent people at the Café were killed and three were wounded. One police officer died an early death, one man went over a balcony and fell twenty stories to his death. One little man died of blade poisoning, one man got his neck broke and one had his throat cut while boating. So you see Miss Geezen you have a lot to answer for.

Jade got her voice back and said. Look, the only person I may have killed was my husband and the law relieved me of that so in essence I didn't kill anyone.

You're going to have to pay Mrs. Geezen, now there are a number of ways you can do this. You can take this knife I have and cut your wrists or you can hang yourself, I'll help you with that. Or you can take this potion in your favorite drink, that's about the most humane I think. No mess, just fall asleep. Last but not least I put a bullet between your evil eyes. I'd love that! You will die this day within the hour let there be no doubt about that, it's just the matter of how you're going to die. What's it going to be Mrs. Geezen?" Willow said?

BREAKING NEWS

Mrs. Jade Geezer was found dead tonight of an apparent drug overdose, she was 44 years old. Mrs. Geezen had been grieving lately because of her husband Robert was killed in a home invasion a few weeks ago. Mrs. Geezen was heavily involved with the "women of the South organization" and "the Southern Arts Ctr." She leaves no known relatives. Mrs. Geezen will surely be missed. Now, for other news...

Willow cut the TV off, finished her drink and went to bed.

Hello Jeff,

Willow said standing at Jeff's door.

'I was wondering what happened to you, Jeff was on crutches and held the door open for her, come on in help yourself to something to drink the bar is over there, I need to get off this hip. Jeff's studio apartment was what she expected, leather couches and chairs, Desk, computer chair large table in front of the couch, La-Z-Boy in which he laid back and drink his tea.

Willow walked over to the bar and poured herself a gin and tonic, and sit down on the couch. The way you are dressed I'd say you're on your way out of town, would I be correct? Jeff said.

 Yes you would, I have to get back to work, and I do have a job you know.

 Well that's what you've been doing down here isn't it? Jeff said.

I mean my real job. Willow said.

I saw the news this morning about the death of Mrs. Geezen. Suicide they called it.

You disagree Jeff? Willow said.

 No, no. Who am I to disagree with the local authorities they never get it wrong. Thad's gone, Mrs. Geezen is gone, I guess I did right to let A.K go, and there is nobody left." Jeff said.

Isn't that great Jeff, now things are back to normal?

Now you can get back to work too!" Willow said.

If I never thanked you I'd like to do it now Jeff

said. Don't forget that money in Pennsylvania that's

waiting for you, it's still there.

I won't Willow said. But!

Is there something else Jeff said? Am I missing

something? If so tell me!

Yes, there is something else I want. "Willow said.

Name it Jeff said. If it's within my power you can

have it.

You! Willow said. I want you!

CHAPTER 5

Janice, I heard you were back in town, how was New Orleans? Jenkins asked. It must have been hot down there how did you stand it? You find anything interesting to do?

Oh, I stayed Busy, sightseeing and toured the old plantations, checked out the Bayou everyone been talking about, did a little gambling. New Orleans is a nice place to visit but I wouldn't want to live there. Maybe if I had went there in January or February doing the Mardi Gras it would have been different.

Yeah, you may be right Janice, well you're back now and I hope ready to go to work. What you got, Willow asked?

Are you still in touch with Dorothy and Jesse?

This will involve them to.

I know how to contact them Willow said. Come to my office tomorrow morning and I'll tell you about it, it'll involve travel.

"Don't they all?" Willow said.

Houston Texas, November 13, 2006, fifth Ward back alley, five in the afternoon. Jesse was trying to pick himself up from just been knocked on his ass by three young men, they found him in one of the men's girlfriend's bed room doing something a man shouldn't be doing to another man's woman. She was leaning over the bed post with her skirt up and panties down. And Jesse was behind her with his pants down to his knees with no room in between. When the men burst through the door Jesse didn't stop until one of the men pulled him off and knocked him down to the floor. "Hey fellas, hey fellas" Jesse said as he was getting up off the floor and pulling his pants up. The guys was stumbling over each other trying to get to Jesse and then the girl fail in between them and they fail over her, thus given Jesse a chance to climb out of the open window and down three stories on the fire escape. Once Jesse was on the ground he started running down the alley. The three men were dead on his ass. After about 50 yards Jesse tripped and twisted his ankle. The men were on him like Jack flash.

They gave him a kick in his ribs, his groin, his head, back and arms.

"Fuck my old lady will you?" one of them said, I'll kill your black ass for that.

And with a dick like yours another one said you not supposed to be fucking nothing.

They beat Jesse what seem like thirty minutes relentlessly until someone said.

"That's enough!"

The guys stopped and looked around to see who was speaking.

There were two very tall black women, both were wearing dark pants suits with wide foster grant sunglasses. Head bandannas and dark blouses, low-cut high heel shoes and a 22 pistol and silencer in their hands.

 There stood Willow and Dorothy.

The men looked at each other and one said to Willow "you sure you want a piece of this?"

Willow shot him in his knee. He screamed and drop to the ground.

 That answer your question?

 The other two men backed away.

 Now, Willow said. Pick your friend up and get the hell out of here.

Jesse, Jesse, Jesse. What the hell have you gotten yourself into this time? Dorothy said. Don't tell me, still can't keep that thing where it belongs can you.

Dorothy, now that wasn't the case, it was where it was supposed to be, Jesse said. It's nice seeing you ladies again but I had the situation well in hand, in another minute or two I would have gotten off this ground and beat their mother jumping asses.

"Jesse, your nose is bleeding," Dorothy said.

"Come on Jesse, we'll help you up," said Willow.

Chapter 6

Three days later in Seoul Korea the team, Willow, Dorothy and Jesse were in the Oconee hotel, room number 1957 having lunch. After Willow had told them of their operation Jesse wanted to know their next step?

"Now, let me get this straight. "Jesse said. Because of my connections we are to infiltrate the drug and prostitute ring. Which has been operating in this area for 50 years or more, I'd say closer to 500 years. Nevertheless, you know you can't stop that shit but can stop the three men at the top. These men hold the key to everything that is everything happening in Seoul. Knock them out and it would make life a lot easier on the lower class and poor, for the moment that is. You know this operation does sound a lot like Simon's, anybody thought of that? We did, Willow said. That was a Different country, different people and whole different scenario.

"An op is an op is an op." Dorothy said.

"Do you know the three people at the head?" Willow asked Jesse.

I think so. Jesse said. There's Renee, A South African got here right after a partied went down, he didn't like what was coming besides he and Kim were friends from way back and Kim convinced him to come to Korea and that was some 10 years ago. I ran into him some five years ago when I left the service so to speak. I even worked for him for a while. Little guy about my size but 10 years my senior. Nice guy on the outside but a killer on the inside. You wouldn't believe the stories I've heard about him. Then there's Kim he's originally Japanese, saw an opening over here doing the Vietnam War and took advantage of it. He loves hashish and the ladies.

Bishop, was straight out of the states. Newark, New Jersey, a stone hood. I heard he killed at least seven people and that includes women. His only loyalty is to Kim and Renée. Not necessarily in that order. He manages the girl because I hear he's gay, Renée and Kim won't trust him with the drugs. Nice looking guy, just a little sweet. Saw him once nothing special that I could see, but you know what they say about that. I hear if he needs something done he has it done mostly by the Chain, the Koran mafia.

And ladies that's about all I know, Jesse said. But we are talking lots of money. By the way Jesse said. What's to be my part this time in all of this?

 You, Willow said are to play the pimp.

 Know you'll like that, Willow said.

Hey, I can do that Jesse said. I do that very well. Where are my stables?

 We are your stable Jesse, Dorothy and I.

Saturday 11:30 PM four days later Willow Jesse and Dorothy walked into the club sea breeze Jesse was in the middle, Willow was on his left and Dorothy on his right. The action stopped for a moment because this was a Korean club and blacks were not known to frequent it. The club was primarily a gambling place but had an area for drinking dancing and lounging. Willow was wearing her hair in a short curl with a flower, ear rings hanging down were snakelike, necklace with a head of a Medusa on it. Her green dress was just above her knees and up to her shoulders, neckline to show maximum breasts with green stilettos. Diamond bracelets on her wrist and rings on her right and left fingers but the one everyone seem to all have their eyes on was her left index finger and the large ring there. A Medusa! Even though this was an Asian country who were used to jewelry like that. Now that takes nerve one lady said. God bless her. Dorothy was dressed just as stunning her shoulder length hair with a string of pearls coming around her forehead the white pearls stood out with her black skin. The dress was of Asian style red up to her neck and down to her knees with a split, high heel shoes that put both her and Willow over 6 feet.

Jesse was in hog heaven at least 3 inches shorter than the ladies in his tuxedo and watch chain hanging from his vest. He said to himself "my bitches". Willow and Dorothy had Jesse by both arms and they walked around the casino, took a glass of champagne from the cocktail waitress, stopped by the crap table and made a few passes. Walked around the club some more with more glances where ever they went. Eventually they pass the lounge and went in. There was a welcome booth and the attendant asked Jesse, a table for three? Before Jesse could answer a young lady of Chinese descent came up to Jesse and said, "Sir. Mr. Renee Táchira asked if you and your party would join him." Jesse looked over to where the girl was pointing, on the far wall of the lounge in a Simi circle booth sat the whole gang under the same roof. Renée, Bishop and Kim–Yon-Lee.

Jesse, it's been a long time. Renée said. They shook hands and Jesse said it has been a long time Renée. And Kim, you still looking good man Jesse said, Bishop just looked at Jesse and nodded his head. What are you doing in Seoul Jesse, business or pleasure?

A little bit of both Renée, I'm glad I caught all of you guys together so we can talk? Besides Renée, Kim and Bishop there were three women in the booth, two Koreans and one Chinese. Renée told them to get up and give their seats to Jesse and the girls. After they were seated Renée said. Okay Jesse let's hear it. But before you start who are these lovely ladies you have with you?

Well, Jesse said pointing to Willow this is Jenny and then pointing to Dorothy this is Ronda they are part of my organization you might say. My private stock you might say.

Well I must say Jesse you sure know how to pick em, now tell me what is it that you want to do.

I'd like to bring my people into Seoul and set up business in your area, all my people are high-class as you can see, commanding a low of $5000-$50,000.

And Jesse tell me this how many associates do you have?

Well only twenty right now but looking to expand to thirty and then maybe fifty.

How many do you plan on putting in Seoul?

To start with only ten Jesse said.

What cities are you in now, Bishop asked? Oson, Osaka, Saigon and Tokyo. We're not talking about low class product as you see and for letting us do business I'm willing to give up 20% of the take from Seoul only that is. Well that's a mouthful Jesse, you don't expect us to decide this tonight do you? Kim asked. Why don't we all just enjoy ourselves have a drink and we'll have an answer for you in the next couple of days Renée said. As he said that he was eyeing Willow, a.k.a. Jenny. On the other side of the booth Kim put his hand on Dorothy's knee.

All that's good Jesse said but I hope you understand there are no freebies here, and my girls are expensive.

Jesse you know money is no object, Renée said. I'll pay whatever it takes.

Willow a.k.a. Jenny asked Dorothy a.k.a. Ronda to go to the ladies room with her. In the ladies room Willow said, can you imagine this, could it have worked out any better than this? I take out Renée and you take out Kim. Perfect!

Okay, but what about Bishop? Dorothy said?

We'll leave him for Jesse. Willow said.

2 AM that morning Willow departed with Renée to his apartment and right after that Kim and Dorothy left.

That left Jesse and Bishop there together and Jesse noticed that Bishop was giving him the eye and had been all night. While dancing earlier Willow had told him that the plan had changed and they were going to make the hits that night but he had to do Bishop.

Bishop was sitting across from Jesse and raised his foot underneath the table over to Jesse's leg and rubbed.

Here we are Bishop said. I always wanted me a black man. There was other things Jesse wanted to say to that but he said "you got one now". On the way over to bishop's apartment, laying in his arms,

Jesse said to himself, the things I do for the team!

CHAPTER 7

The sex was great I couldn't have asked for better,

the touch in the right places the feeling just where I

like it. I didn't have to tell her where to go and what

to do as you have to with so many these days, she

just knew. Now this was heaven it don't get any

better than this. Early-morning sex 5:30 AM and

she doesn't have to be at work until nine, plenty of

time for round three. Maybe four. Willow laid back

breathing hard and caressing Bobby's breasts.

Bobby an airline stewardess with her back to

Willow put her hand on hers and breathed a sigh of contentment, both were very happy. Until!

 Willow all of the sudden became very rigid, her body got stiff, feet felt like they were extending along with fingers and nails. Her Eyes were starting to get wide, nose and mouth getting wider. Teeth growing outside her lips, Neck getting longer and hair moving on its own like there is something live up there. Then Willow knew what it was, exactly what it was.

"It "had come back, the feeling that has come back on her all of her life and she never knew when. She equates it to the Medusa feeling, whenever she gets this feeling she knows one thing, she is about to kill somebody, anybody. But she didn't want to kill this one, she didn't want to harm this one so she jumped

out of bed put on her shorts, halter and running

shoes. Bobby looked at her and asked where she

was going at 5:30 in the morning?

You know I run Willow said, I just got the feeling

to run.

Hold on a minute and I'll go with you Bobby said.

No, you get your rest, after all you have your flight

in a few hours. Besides Willow thought, I don't

want to hurt you. Willow left out the apartment and

then the hotel within five minutes and started

running at a fast pace headed toward the park.

That afternoon after she returned from her run, and

after Bobby had left for her flight Willow was

sitting out on her patio having lunch of a Shrimp Salad with blue cheese and an iced tea.

She must really learn how to control "it" she thought, that was a close one. The problem is that she never know when it's coming out. But then there are times when she was with those she really didn't mind killing, but not this one, not bobby. After lunch Willow went back in the apartment retrieved her a bottle of water from the fridge, picked up the TV remote and turned on the local news.

BREAKING NEWS

Earlier today a lady jogger was found dead in the local park with her throat slashed, she was found underneath a bridge leading to the street. She was wearing jogger shorts, shoes and halter. Whistle around her neck but no purse or fanny pack. No suspects for the killing at this time. Joggers often run in that area in early mornings and late at night. Her identity is not known.

Now, for other news...

Hello Janice this is agent stone, how's it going?

How you enjoying the West Coast, Tacoma Washington isn't it?

Yes, willow said. Why you asked, you know already.

Well I was just trying to be nice.

Agent stone was the assistant agent in charge of the FBI under agent Jenkins the head of the section. This unit was unique in that the office they were in held the FBI, Homeland security, NSA and CIA. All these agencies in one, they finally decided to work together. It's been three years now and a number of operations together but still no sign of them letting me off the hook, Willow thought. The agency knew about this little problem I have and they decided to use it for themselves. I think it worked out pretty good for them and for me seeing as though I'm still doing what I want to do and I'm not in jail.

What can I do for you agent stone?

Since you finished that last assignment so quick we have another for you.

That last assignment was just luck agent stone, that won't happen again.

Maybe not; but you and the team carried it out and in good fashion, I might add. Everyone here is very pleased with the outcome. Also the Cleveland operation and the New Orleans job was all well done.

New Orleans? What do you know about New Orleans? Willow asked?

Please Janice, we know everything, we are the FBI you know.

I guess I forgot. Willow said.

Please, don't do that Janice, please!

Now, you're close to McCord Air Force Base right outside of Tacoma. There is a plane waiting for you at hangar number 11, tail number 756, a Learjet. They're expecting you.

Will I need Dorothy and Jesse for this one? I shouldn't think so but if you do feel free to bring them in.

45,000 feet in the air, 4 p.m. in the afternoon a Thursday Willow was conversing with stone on the planes phone.

Janice, this is what we have!

A whistle blower showed up and started talking about this prostitution ring, during one break in our session she was waylaid from lunch and beat up pretty bad. She's in a coma as we speak. What we did get out of her is that the prostitution ring she spoke of are all women in the military, Air Force to be exact and it's at a high level. A couple of colonels are involved we're told, the headquarters is at Lack land Air Force Base in San Antonio Texas. But it's not exclusively in Texas there are six other bases in other states and countries around the world that may be involved. Your job is to infiltrate this ring and if possible burst it up. And Janice you'll be going back in the service for this one.

Chapter 8

Willow reported to the 4395 transportation squadron Lack land Air Force Base Texas on Monday, 15 November 2000. She was wearing the rank of Master Sgt., in air force dress blues plus ribbons on her left chest.

Kuwait liberation medal, united nations metal, Kuwait liberation medal Kingdom of Saudi Arabia, AF for exemplary service ribbon, Korea defenses service medal, global war on terrorism service medal, South West Asia service medal, Iraq campaign medal, Afghanistan Campaign Medal, Air Force recognition Medal, outstanding airmen of the year with oak leaf cluster, good conduct medal with silver oak leaf cluster, , Air Force outstanding unit award, Air Force commendation medal, Purple Heart, Air Force achievement medal.

 With Her briefcase on her lap, she was sitting in the orderly room waiting to go in and speak to the squadron commander. The office consisted of two other females and two males of which one of them was being shipped out, Willow would be his replacement. The two WAF's (women air force) were a Sgt. and staff Sgt. respectfully. The men were a two striper and a master Sgt. the master Sgt. is who she would be replacing. The C.O. Finally called her into his office, he was an older type major. Gray hair placed on heavy jaws in the face. He had a look like he hadn't shaved that day or the last few days really. Heavy around the middle,

Stone boozer Willow guessed. When they get that old without being promoted Willow knew that he was at the end of his term with the military. He's out to pasture now and he has to know that. I'll check his records when I get a chance just to see if I'm right. He goes through the spill of welcoming me to the squadron. Hoping I enjoy my stay. I'll be replacing the outgoing section leader he'll be here just long enough to train her and on and on. If I need anything his door is always open.

Damn, she was glad she was out of all this bull shit.

Two weeks later after work Willow was on her way to her quarters when one of the girls, Lisa asked if she wanted to go over to the club for a drink?

Willow told her sure but she would have to drive, my car is on the blink. I want be able to have it fixed till next payday. Lisa the staff Sgt. who worked with her asked if she'd like to borrow a few dollars to tie her over. Willow told her no thanks, she doesn't like owing anyone.

At the club Willow ordered a gin tonic and Lisa ordered a rum and coke. After a few drinks and small talk Lisa said. Willow I know you're tight for money I've assume you are having problems with your car maybe I can help.

I've told you before Lisa I want borrow any money from you.

No, you won't have to do that, suppose I were to tell you how you could make your own money in little or no time. That is if you're open to it.

How much money are we talking about and what do I have to do? Willow asked.

Let's say $1500 a night. Is that something you would be interested in? Lisa asked.

Tell me more Willow said, I am in need of money as you know, and that do sound nice. What can I earn on the high-end?

With your looks and all I'd say you could go for somewhere around 2500 dollar's. The only way I know you can make that kind of money is…
Willow let it trail off.

Is that what we're talking about Lisa? Maybe.

Maybe not. But if we were would you be

interested?

"I don't know." Willow said. I'm surely not above

something like that, I'll have to think on it. Give me

a few days. One question though? How would I

know for sure about the money?

 You'll have to talk to someone else about that other

than me but from where I'm sitting there'll be no

problems. Let me know when you're ready.

Agent stone this is Janice, I made contact with the

people. The girl that works with me (Lisa)

approached me about making some money and

quite a bit of money I might add. Lisa says I have

to talk to someone else before I am confirmed but

I'm sure it's on. I'll call you back in a few days

that's when I told Lisa I'd make my decision.

Janice, watch yourself these people don't play

around. The whistleblower that was in a coma, she

just died!

A week later. At the Hotel Bowie in San Antonio,

Texas. At 7:45 PM off the dining room Willow was

at the bar, she was told that she would be met by

someone at approximately 8 PM. Willow was

wearing a plain black dress very little

makeup(although she didn't need any) and medium

high heels. She wore a String of white pearls, hair

straight back with a small purse. She had a Gin and

tonic in front of her with a cherry on top. 8 PM and

no one showed up, 8:15, no one showed. At 8:45

when she was preparing to leave a person came up to her and offered to buy her a drink.

"I was about to leave, maybe another time." Willow said.

You don't want to go just yet Sgt Willow, we should talk.

The man speaking to her was a person that she had seen before, at the club, she thought an older chief Master Sgt. about ready to retire with close to 30 years' service she figured. But this night he was wearing civilian clothes, a black sports coat, white dress shirt open at the collar and blue jeans. His shoes were the hush puppy type slip on. He had Black hair with gray mix on the sides. Black eyes and black and gray mustache. He also was black.

"You know my name but I don't know yours.

Willow said.

"My name is Sgt. Manning but you can call me

Robert. Have you had dinner yet?" Robert asked.

I think the dining room is about to close isn't it

Willow said.

They never close, not this hotel, it's the clientele

they have. They won't allow it, of course they pay

for it. Let's go, our table is waiting. During dinner

Robert and Willow made small talk about her job

and where she was stationed before she got to

Lackland. How long she had been in the service,

was she going to retire? The basic questions one

military person says to another. Then Robert asked,

what all did Lisa tell her about what we do?

She told me that I could make from 1500 to 2500 in one night and I guessed what I would have to do for that kind of money. She never said anything about the where, who and when. She said someone else would tell me that, are you that someone Robert?

I am! We give a service to people who are looking for companionship to those out of town visitors. Be it men or women as long as they can pay. And as you can imagine they pay very well. This hotel has over 2000 rooms and they're not cheap. The cheapest go's around $1800 per night on up to $50,000 a night. So you see the residents are use to the best. That brings up what they expect in the product they get, it has to be top of the line. We think you'll fit in that line. Lisa was right, 1500 just to start but you will make considerable more than that. Any questions?

How do I get in touch with these clients, is that what you call them? And how do I go about collecting my money? You will collect no money it will be collected for you before you meet the clients. The price will be set if there is something extra these clients want then that'll be up to you. Sometime they'll give you a tip, that's yours. This is one of the reasons why the split is 70-30.

That's kind of high isn't it, Willow said.

It is but you'll make it up on your tips, we've heard some of the girls get more than the set price. Does that sound like something you'd like to do? Robert said. Sound's good. Willow said. When do I start?

I'm going to need some bills upfront, I guess you've

heard about my automobile. I know that's not your

problem but I do need a way to get here.

No problem Janice, may I call you Janice? We'll

leave the last names for the base.

By the way Janice asked, you do screen your

clients don't you?

Janice; we know everyone that comes in here. If

not by name then by referral.

And my first date is when?

Lisa will let you know Robert said.

CHAPTER 9

Agent stone, I met with the second link in the chain his name is Robert Manning and he's a master Sgt., he works at base headquarters. He may be the one that sets up the dates but I don't think so I'd start with the head clerk, he would know the entire goings on in the hotel or the manager may be even better.

Janice we have people down there covering your back and will be looking into Robert Manning. Did you have a look at your squadron C.O.?

Yes I did Janice said and we can forget about him, he spends most of his time in the officer's club. I checked his desk one night and found two fifths of Jim Beam.

I see you got your car fixed Lisa said, I guess I won't have to drive you over to the club after work anymore.

No Janice said I'll be able to make it on my own, see you there.

Janice we have a date for you, Saturday at 9 PM, Room 1325, Lisa sipped her drink, is there any questions?

"Dress code?" Willow said.

Up to you Lisa said. Just think of you going out on a date. How do you know I'm the type of woman they're looking for Willow asked.

When they get to the desk they tell our girl their preference, she'll come up with the woman and the price. Always high and it will be taken off their credit card right then. And how is this tip handled? Tips are Handled the same way; but the next morning.

Have you ever been stiffed? Willow asked. Two years of doing this, never!

That' Saturday at 9 PM at Room number 1325 Willow knocked lightly on the door. A muffled voice came through the door, come on in its open. Willow walked in and the voice came out the bathroom, be right with you. Willow thought she knew that voice. All of a sudden Jesse walked out of the room. HI BABE! He says. Trick-or-treat.

Jesse! What the hell are you doing here? (All the while giving him a big hug).

Stone thought you might need a little help on this one.

So I was right there in Houston so he called me in. I think you might be growing on the old boy for him to call me. How you doing? Jesse said.

I'm fine Jesse, I guess you know about the operation I'm on?

Yes I do and guess who the client is?

How did you and stone pull that one off? Willow asked.

Well after you told stone about the setup I just hi-tailed it over here and told the clerk what I was looking for and WA-LA here you are. Paid some

good money for you I want you to know.

Don't forget the tip Willow said.

I haven't seen you since that night in the club, what

happened with you and Bishop? Well if you must

know, right after you ladies left Bishop Hit on me

and since you two decided to change the plan I

thought my best bet was to go along with him. It

was hard because what I have is for the ladies not

for the men. After reaching his apartment he just

about tore my clothes off, I told him to hold on a

minute that I had to go to the bathroom. You know

I keep this Walter P–22 in an ankle holster, so once

in the bathroom I pulled it out. I Came out the door

with a towel draped around the muzzle and put

three rounds in him and one in the head, just like we were train to do. Never want to go through that again.

How you coming on this operation Jesse asked? You are step number four, number one was Lisa, and number two is a guy named Robert Manning and number three the clerk at the front desk. Next we need to know who is in charge of this whole operation.

"Well I can cover you for tonight Janice but after this you'll be on your own." Jesse said. I think I may be able to get a few more days out of this, after all I am supposed to be here on business.

I can handle it Janice said. Do you have anything to drink around here?

A gin and tonic would be nice!

You know Janice I could try to keep you exclusively, say I'm so overwhelmed with you I want to keep you for as long as I'm in town. Keep you from the lowlife.

I don't know Jesse that may slow us down from getting the guy at the top. And as far as the low life's; their far from that. We'll do this tonight, and see where it goes from here.

You know Jesse I'm halfway looking for Dorothy to pop up.

That Monday morning (early) at work Lisa approach Janice and said, how did your week end go?

I couldn't have asked for better Janice said. What they call a piece of cake.

There is something coming to you later on today and what I hear quite the prize. The ones in the know says they haven't seen a tip like that in quite a while. It matches the set price and more. Damn, what did you put on this guy?

Lisa, I learned this over life. When you go out to do something you give it all you got. Janice said. What do you know about this guy anyway? Janice asked.

He was a referral, and is in the hip-hop business backing people like heavy D, Jay-Z and Beyoncé,

Usher and boys to men, People like that. He's loaded.

He's supposed to be in town another week so you may get another shot at him.

That'll work. Janice said.

Oh, I almost forgot someone would like to meet you. Lisa said.

And who would that be?

Someone high up in the bird range, I think your true potential is being known Janice. Are we talking about more money? Because money is all I'm interested in.

I'd say so, I'll let you know. Lisa said.

Base headquarters Wednesday 1430 hrs. (The base commander's outer office)

The base commander will see you now the secretary said.

A rather young man in his early 40s, full head of hair, he was clean-shaven and no mustache. He was 6 feet one, 220 pounds. Dress Blues with an Eagle on each shoulder. He was sitting behind a large desk with the American flag on his right and national flag on his left. His Name plate said Col. Jackson B. Beaver base commander.

Willow walked up to the desk and gave him a salute and did the at ease thing. Feet apart, hands behind the back, hand in hand.

At ease Sgt Willow and please have a seat. After sitting in one of the large overstuffed lounge chairs, the Col. brought out a folder with Willows name on it and started to look it over but Willow knew he had already done that.

Sgt. Willow you've had quite a career I see. Korea, Afghanistan, Kuwait, and Germany. Numerous awards and accommodations and up for another promotion, you seem to excel with whatever you do.

"I try" Willow said.

The job you were on this weekend was what I would call over the top, I like that.

I'm sure I don't know what you're talking about, would you like to enlighten me. Willow said.

Sgt. Willow I am the base commander, I know everything that goes on around my base and I know what goes on with you.

Sgt. Willow you're a very beautiful woman a lot of men will give a lot to have you as evident by the compensation you received this weekend. I think it can continue but at another level.

And what would that level be? Willow asked.

There is a congressman coming into town this weekend that's on the committee on base closings, he loves your type of woman, I think he'll like you.

I don't understand, maybe you could spell it out for me. Willow said.

Okay, the client you entertained this past weekend, I'm asking you to do it again with the congressman.

Col. seeing as though we're on the same page, I thought Sgt. Manning was to be my middleman. Willow said.

Normally he is but this is a little too big for Sgt. Manning and it just came up. I decided to handle this one myself.

All that's good sir but I haven't gotten paid for the last job. I was told I'd get paid two, three days ago.

I'm sorry about that Sgt. Willow that was my fault. I wanted to hold off on giving you your "extra" until I had a chance to have this talk with you. The

Col. pushed a business type envelope across the desk toward Willow and she stood up and retrieved it. Felt the size of it but didn't count it.

Better? The Col. said.

Yes, better. Willow said.

You were saying something about a congressman? Willow said.

This Saturday you'll accompany him for dinner, maybe a show and the rest of the evening.

Money? Willow said?

60/40. The Col. said plus the "extras". Twice what you receive the last time, this one is really important.

Col. as long as the extras are there you can depend on me.

And Sgt. Willow from now on you'll bypass Sgt. Manning and come directly to me, for the next six months anyway.

 Yes Sir Willow said.

Back in her car and in the parking lot of the base bowling alley

Willow pulled out the Minnie USB recorder checked it out and called agent stone.

It's all coming together Janice, your man Robert Manning has been under surveillance for some time now and there is at least 10 more women he's controlling, we can pick him up at any time. Lisa, the girl that works with you also have the girls she's working on a smaller scale, Out of the NCO club.

The hotel desk clerk and two others are there.

Looks like the colonel is the top dog and with that tape you got us we have his ass. Now to reel in this congressman, once he pays for sex we got him. The other bases are on track to come down at about the same time, for right now you take care.

 When do you anticipate picking everyone up? Janice asked

Saturday right after the congressmen signed his credit card statement acknowledging what he's signing for.

And what about my tip Willow said?

Now Janice stone said.

 Just joking, Janice said, just joking!

CHAPTER 10

It was Saturday afternoon at approximately 1700 hrs. (5 PM) Lisa and Janice was sitting together at the NCO club, having their usual.

Big date tonight? Lisa said.

 You could say that. Janice said. Give me a chance to get rid of that old heap I have and get me something decent.

 What are you thinking about buying, nothing flashy I hope?" Lisa said.

 Nothing like drawing fly's to you by having flashy stuff. Cars, jewelry and expensive things.

No, nothing like that, Janice said. Maybe something low-key like a two or three year old Ford, Mazda or Toyota.

"I think you do know how to play the game Janice" Lisa said.

"Talking about playing the game I have to get out of here, I have a date tonight you know" Janice said.

"Get em' girl" Lisa said.

As Janice was leaving the table a Sgt. was watching them from across the room and did a double take at Janice. He felt that he knew her, had seen her before. Korea, Kuwait or Germany maybe. Lisa he knew but only to hit on her a time or two, maybe this time would be the charm. He walked over to Lisa's table and asked if he could buy her a drink? Lisa was in a pretty good mood and the guy looked decent enough so she said yes.

After all it was a Saturday and she was off (both jobs) tonight. But then again she was never off her second job, there in the club. The ones in the know, they know who to come to if they want a "date". This Sgt. hadn't been here all that long so he had no clue. His name tag said T. Booker and she ordered her usual, rum and Coke and he started shooting the same old bull shit that all men do before trying to get into a girl's pants (for free). Then the conversation turned toward the girl that was sitting at the table with her, Janice. He thought he knew her from somewhere.

Maybe Lisa said. She's been in the service almost 15 years now and been around. Korea, Kuwait, Germany.

That's where I've seen her before but the girl I remember left Germany unexpectedly and I heard was discharged.

Well that had to be wrong, Lisa said, because as you can see she's right here in uniform and in person.

Yeah, I guess you're right because I also heard that after she was discharged the feds picked her up and hired her.

Lisa had her drink up to her lips and when she heard that she dropped the drink and started shaking, eyes bugged and mouth open. And ask

Booker to repeat what he just said? And asked was he sure about that.

Janice Willow, I could never forget a woman like that. I also heard she's gay.

Tell me more of what you heard while in Germany. Lisa said.

Booker told of her not hanging out with anyone in particular, men or women, knew of no study bow. Went to town a lot, heard she party with the Germans. One day she got called up to the base commander's office and a day later someone saw her at the flight line boarding a Learjet with no markings. That's been about three years ago.

I have to go Booker, thanks for the drink. I'm sure I'll see you again. Lisa stood up and just about ran out the club.

That mother F, Lisa said. That mother F. Lisa was half a block from Janice quarters when she saw her get into her car and drive toward the main gate. She was dressed to kill and that's exactly what Lisa intended to do to her. She was glad that she was leaving the base, didn't want to do her there.

Lisa stayed three car lengths behind her, didn't want to get too close, after all she knew her car. Janice happened to glance in her rearview mirror and thought she saw Lisa about three car lengths back, I wonder what she's up to Janice thought.

Lisa had called Robert and told him what she was told and what she was going to do. Robert told her not to do anything that he would take care of it but Lisa told him forget that, she was going to do her because of the fool she made of her and then she hung up.

He tried to call her back but she never picked up, the message went straight to voicemail. Robert called the two men he had in his employment and told them the situation. Get her away from the Congressman and find a quiet place to off her. I don't want to hear of her body being found even on the late-night news.

Janice pulled into the underground garage and she watched Lisa follow her in so she parked in the rear area furthest from the elevator. When Lisa exit her own car she looked around for Janice, no Janice. She pulled out her Smith& Wesson MP9 and tipped up to Janice's Car with both hands on the trigger ready to fire. No Janice! Until…… Janice came up behind her and put her knife to her throat. "You want to tell me what this is all about Lisa?" Janice said.

You know got damn well what this is about, COP.

How'd you find that out? Janice said.

Someone saw you and pointed you out, your ass is grass Janice. I've already told Robert and he'll have someone here in no time. I'm just sorry I didn't get the chance to put a bullet in your mother F head myself. Go ahead, call your buddies, and lock me up. Do what you people do. But I'll be out one day and that'll be your ass.

Lisa. You misunderstand, I don't do the arrest thing, and I'm not the one. Then she cut Lisa's throat from ear to ear.

Damn girl, you show took care of that! Jesse! What the hell are you doing here?

Agent stone again, he thought you may need backup. I've been here in this garage for over an hour now. What you want to do with old girl here?

Put her in her own trunk, its right over there. Janice said.

How did she get on to you, Jesse asked? Someone from my past ratted me out, it happens. Now I have to get to the Congressman.

After calling his two men about Janice Sgt. Manning tried to call Col. Beaver but only got his voicemail. He then called the area he was having a meeting in that was top-secret but all cell phones had been confiscated. Then the knock came at his door.

The Congressman was at the Desk when Janice emerge from the garage elevator having been told who he was Janice made a B-turn toward him. After signing for his credit card Janice was next to him and he smiled and said, right on time.

He noticed how she was dressed and his mouth started watering and his lions started swelling and he said, why don't we forgo the show for tonight and go directly up to my room?

"Whatever you say Congressman" Janice said.

At the elevator two men came up to them, one on each side of Janice and told both there's been a change in plans. One took the Congressman by the arm and walked him away and the other continue holding on to Janice. When the elevator arrived and the door opened; there was one lady passenger already inside to the rear. Buttons for the 20th floor had already been pushed. Janice and the hit man entered the elevator and turn around facing the door with their backs to the lady.

The hit man press floor number 19 with his left hand because the knife he was holding on Janice was in his right and into her rib cage. No one said a word as they were going up. Not Janice or the hit

man nor the lady. Until!

They reached the 19th floor and the door opened

and Janice and the hit man started to walk out that's

when Dorothy shot him in the back of the head.

Dorothy, Janice said. I was wondering when you

were going to show up.

 Now, you know Janice when agent stone called

Jesse he's going to call me to. We are a team!

Three days later at another hotel in San Antonio,

room number 1456, Willow, Dorothy and Jesse

was sitting down having a drink hashing over what

went on the last few weeks. The Col. was picked up

in Washington DC outside the meeting he was in.

Sgt. Robert Manning was picked up at his quarters

but not before he had made the call to the two hit

man, which was caught on tape. Lisa had not been

found as of yet, and assumed to have gone AWOL.

The clerks at the hotel were all picked up and

readily confessed to their role in the conspiracy.

The congressman was also picked up with the hit

man who was charged only with having a weapon

by a felon. There was talk of another hit man but he

was never found. The bases fail one after the other

with one brigadier general being brought down in

the Malay. What an operation. Jesse said. But all

and all everything turned out O.K...

 Well, what's next Dorothy said?

A toast! Willow said.

To the team!

To the team! The others said.

www.ingramcontent.com/pod-product-compliance
Lightning Source LLC
Chambersburg PA
CBHW060424260626
47161CB00005B/1779